# APPLES, APPLES, ALL YEAR ROUND

## A CELEBRATION OF JEWISH HOLIDAYS

By Barbara Bietz and June Sobel

Illustrated by Ruth Waters

APPLES & HONEY PRESS

For friends and family, who make life sweet, all year round. – BB

For Adam and Xiaoyin, a life as sweet as apples dipped in honey. – JS

For Sam and Poppy. – RW

Apples & Honey Press
An Imprint of Behrman House Publishers
Millburn, New Jersey 07041
www.applesandhoneypress.com

ISBN 978-1-68115-595-1

Library of Congress Cataloging-in-Publication Data

Names: Bietz, Barbara, author. | Sobel, June, author.
Title: Apples, apples, all year round : a celebration of Jewish holidays / by Barbara Bietz and June Sobel.
Description: Millburn, New Jersey : Apples & Honey Press, [2022] | Audience: Ages 2-3. | Audience: Grades K-1. | Summary: "A tour through Jewish holidays, with apples as the lens"-- Provided by publisher.
Identifiers: LCCN 2021050268 | ISBN 9781681155951 (hardback)
Subjects: CYAC: Stories in rhyme. | Apples--Fiction. | Fasts and feasts--Judaism--Fiction. | Jews--Fiction. | LCGFT: Picture books. | Stories in rhyme.
Classification: LCC PZ8.3.B474 Ap 2022 | DDC [E]--dc23
LC record available at https://lccn.loc.gov/2021050268

Design by Alexandra N. Segal
Edited by Aviva Lucas Gutnick
Printed in China

9 8 7 6 5 4 3 2 1

0822/B1892/A1

# Apples! Apples!

Apples, apples,
all year round,
juicy, fresh, and yummy.

Apples, apples,
sweet new year,
apples dipped in honey.

Apples, apples,
stars above,
apple cake to eat.

Apples, apples,
wave your flag,
candy apple treat.

Apples, apples,
latkes hot,
applesauce for me.

Apples, apples,
have a bite,
time to plant a tree.

Apples, apples,
baskets full,
let's all celebrate.

Apples, apples,
chopped with nuts,
for our seder plate.

Apples, apples,
gooey good,
blintzes in my tummy.

Apples, apples,
all year round,
juicy, fresh, and yummy!